P9-CKF-975

WITHDRAWN

To my sister, Pamela, who has always shown the way.
– O.C.

To all of those who, from time to time, need some encouragement for their own journey of discovery.
– J.A.

immedium
Immedium, Inc.  P.O. Box 31846  San Francisco, CA 94131
www.immedium.com

Text Copyright ©2006 Oliver Chin
Illustrations Copyright ©2006 Jeremiah Alcorn

All rights reserved, including the right of reproduction in whole or in part in any form.
For information about special discounts for bulk purchases, please contact Immedium Special Sales at sales@immedium.com.

First hardcover edition (ISBN 978-1-59702-007-7) published 2006.

Edited by Don Menn
Book design by Elaine Chu & Dorothy Mak
Chinese translation by Hsiaoying Chen, Grace Mak and Dorothy Mak
Calligraphy by Lucy Chu

Printed in Malaysia
10 9 8 7 6 5 4 3 2 1

Names: Chin, Oliver Clyde, 1969- author. | Alcorn, Miah, illustrator.
Title: The year of the pig : tales from the Chinese zodiac / written by Oliver Chin ; illustrated by Miah Alcorn.
Description: [Revised edition.] | San Francisco : Immedium, Inc., [2019] | In English and simplified Chinese. | Summary: Patty the piglet learns what her best qualities really are when Farmer Wu needs everyone's help to find a lost ring. Lists the birth years and characteristics of individuals born in the Chinese Year of the Pig.
Identifiers: LCCN 2018014286 (print) | LCCN 2018021000 (ebook) | ISBN 9781597021456 (ebook) | ISBN 9781597021432 (hardcover)
Subjects: | CYAC: Pigs--Fiction. | Animals--Infancy--Fiction. | Domestic animals--Fiction. | Astrology, Chinese--Fiction. | Chinese language materials--Bilingual.
Classification: LCC PZ10.831 (ebook) | LCC PZ10.831 .C6154 2018 (print) | DDC [E]--dc23
LC record available at https://lccn.loc.gov/2018014286

# The Year of the Pig

## Tales from the Chinese Zodiac

十二生肖故事系列 猪年的故事

**Written by Oliver Chin**
**Illustrated by Miah Alcorn**

文： 陈曜豪
图： 艾尔康祖曼亚

immedium
Immedium, Inc.
San Francisco. CA

At dawn, a joyful squeal rang through the farmyard.
A new day had just begun, so Farmer Wu woke up and walked out to his barn. Inside Mama and Papa Pig just had a baby!

黎明时分，一阵快乐的尖叫声响遍整个农场。
新的一天刚开始，农夫老吳醒来往外面谷仓走去，
発現猪妈妈和猪爸爸刚生了一只猪宝宝！

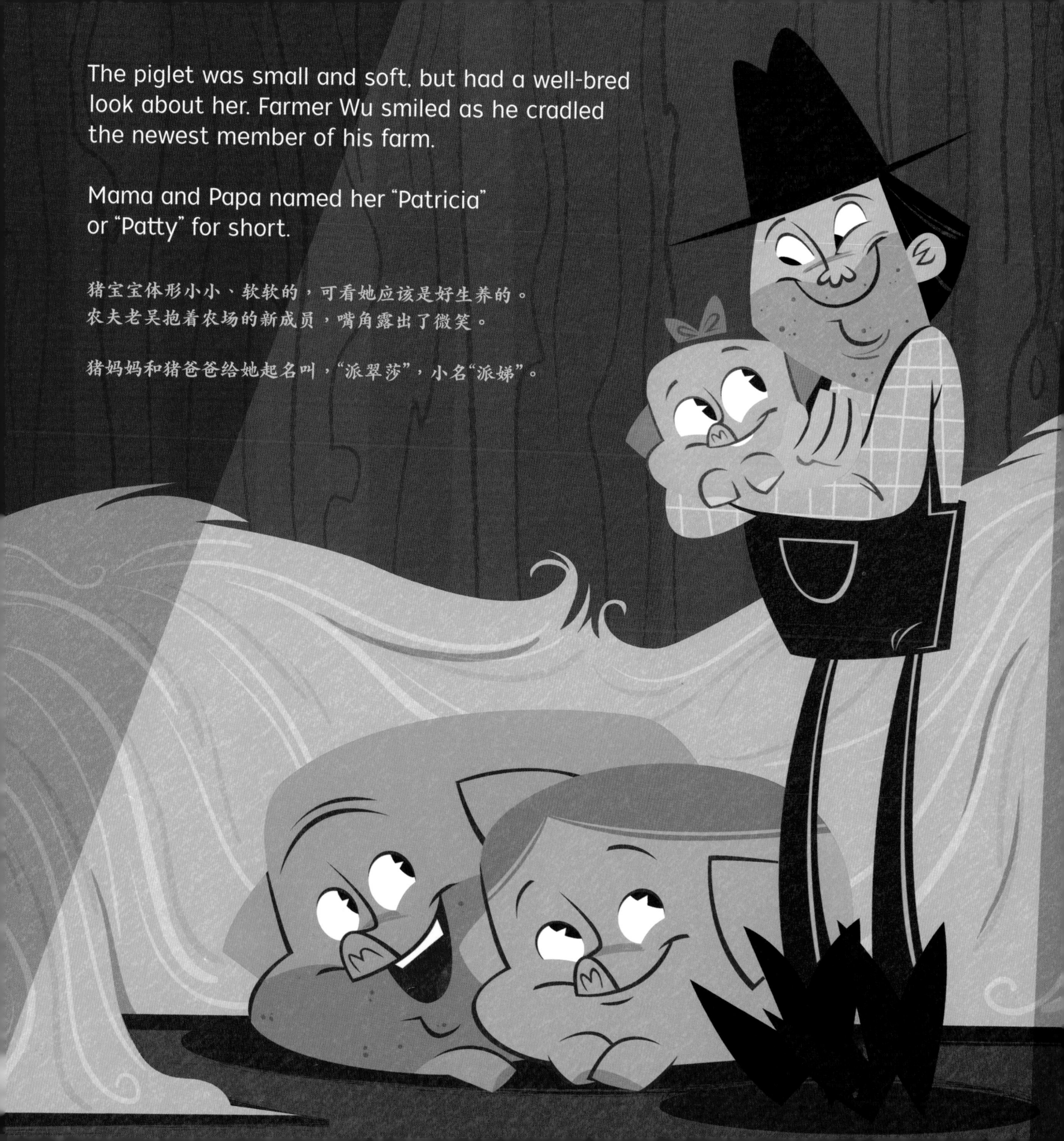

The piglet was small and soft, but had a well-bred look about her. Farmer Wu smiled as he cradled the newest member of his farm.

Mama and Papa named her "Patricia" or "Patty" for short.

猪宝宝体形小小、软软的，可看她应该是好生养的。
农夫老吴抱着农场的新成员，嘴角露出了微笑。

猪妈妈和猪爸爸给她起名叫，"派翠莎"，小名"派娣"。

All the neighbors wanted to see the baby.
Big and small, they crowded around the pigpen.
They congratulated Mama and Papa and
cooed at little Patty.

所有的邻居都想看看猪宝宝。大大小小全挤在猪圈周围。
他們向猪妈妈和猪爸爸祝贺，又忙着逗弄派娣。

Mama whispered in Patty's ear,
"These are your uncles, aunts,
and cousins."

猪妈妈在派娣耳边低语:
"这些是你的叔叔，阿姨和表哥们。"

Papa added, "Listen to your elders,
because they know what is best for you."

猪爸爸补充说："妳要听长辈的话，
因为他们知道什么对你是最好的。"

Delighted, Patty clapped her hooves, **"Yay!"**

派娣高兴地拍拍她的蹄子，"好极了！"

Quickly Patty learned the lay of the land. Mama showed her where the farmer's family and the other animals lived. Then Papa taught her all their names and duties.

派娣很快就熟悉了农场的环境。猪妈妈向她介绍了农夫的家人和其他动物住的地方。然后爸爸教她认识动物的名字和工作。

Everyone admired how Patty was such a fast learner.

**"What's next for me to study?"** Patty asked eagerly.

So a few of them agreed that it was time to teach her some manners.

大家都很佩服派娣学习得又快又好。
"接下来我要学什么？"派娣迫切地问。
有些动物认为是时候要教她一些规矩。

Patty's parents liked to roll in the mud, especially to cool off on hot days. Next door, Auntie Sheep shook her head and advised Patty, "You should keep your skin clean, just like my wool."

派娣的父母喜欢在泥巴里打滚，在大热天里特别能消暑。
隔壁的羊阿姨摇头说："你应该保持皮肤清洁，就像我的羊毛一样。"

and sitting on the soft wet earth.
Nothing felt better than a good mud bath!

"这样脏兮兮的很有趣啊，"派娣回答。她很享受翻滚！滑倒！
坐在软软的泥巴里。没什麼比洗一个泥巴浴更棒了！

Mama and Papa loved mealtime when Farmer Wu would fill their trough. Nearby, Uncle Ox flicked his tail and instructed Patty, "You should chew slowly and not make a mess."

吃饭的时候，猪妈妈和猪爸爸最喜欢农夫老吴把饲料槽填得满满。旁边的牛叔叔轻轻地拍着他的尾巴，吩附派娣说:“吃饭的时候你应该慢慢咀嚼，不要吃得这么肮脏。”

**"But food smells too tasty,"** explained Patty.

"可是食物的味道实在太香了，"派娣解释。

When she got hungry, Patty hurried to join her parents and dived face first into her chow.

当她饿了的时候，派娣趕緊加入她父母的行列，
然後将整个脸埋進食物堆里。

After every meal, Patty looked very sloppy indeed.

每次吃完饭后，看派娣的樣子都是非常邋遢。

At night, Patty's parents nestled beside each other and snored loudly. Auntie Horse pawed at the ground and told Patty, "You should sleep standing up and not be so noisy."

晚上，派娣的父母总是挨在一起睡觉和大声打鼾。
马阿姨轻轻地踏踏地，告诉派娣:“你应该站着睡觉，
不要打呼。”

**"But laying down feels so good,"**
sighed Patty.

At bedtime, Patty would always squeeze in between her parents. Warm and snug, Patty would slumber up a storm.

"躺着睡可舒服啊，"派娣叹口气说。

睡觉了，派娣总是挤在父母的中间。
她感觉舒服又暖和，派娣也会发出如雷声的鼾声。

Patty liked her pigpen. But other animals got to wander about the farm, and Patty wanted to explore as well.

She nudged the gate with her snout, but it wouldn't budge.

派娣都喜欢她的猪圈。但她看见其它动物在农场里徘徊，她也想探索一下。

於是用鼻子碰一碰栅栏，可惜栅栏动也不动。

Strolling by, Cousin Dog grinned
and shook his head.

He warned her, "Be content to stay where
you are and leave the roaming to others."

Patty snorted in disagreement
and curled her tail.

狗表哥缓缓走过来，看了看派娣摇摇头笑了。

他警告她:“你还是好好地待着吧！
别想跟其他的动物四处徘回。”

派娣不服气地哼了一声，卷起她的尾巴。

Then one morning, Farmer Wu shouted, "Ai Ya! Where did it go?"

He had lost his valuable jade ring!

Soon the whole farm buzzed with excitement.

一天早上，传来农夫老吴的大叫声：
“哎呀！去了哪里呢？“

他弄丢了自己宝贵的玉戒指！

很快地這个消息传遍了整个农场。

Patty rooted around the pen,
but didn't find anything.

Cousin Dog laughed, "Don't worry.
This is my job, so just sit back and watch."

派娣找遍了整个猪圈，还是找不到东西。
狗表哥笑着说:“别担心，这是我的工作，看我吧！“

Off Cousin Dog went. He sniffed Farmer Wu's hand and began hunting for the missing jade ring.

Patty shouted, **"I want to help too!"**
But she could only watch anxiously from her pigpen.

狗表哥离开了。他嗅了嗅农夫老吴的手，
开始寻找失踪的玉戒指。

派娣喊叫："我也想帮忙！"
她只能在猪圈里干焦急看着。

All day long, Farmer Wu and Cousin Dog ran around the farm.
Patty thought, **"I bet they will find his ring soon."**

But alas, after a long day of looking,
they had no luck!

农夫老吴和狗表哥整天在农场走来走去。
派娣想:"我打赌他们很快找到玉戒指。"

唉！可是找了一整天，還是找不到！

The following day, Patty saw Farmer Wu search the fields on Auntie Horse.

第二天，派娣看到农夫老吴骑着马阿姨找遍整个田野。

Then his wife scoured the stream on Uncle Ox.

而他的妻子骑着牛叔叔在小河里搜寻。

Even his son combed through Auntie Sheep's wool.

甚至他的儿子也在正梳理羊阿姨的羊毛来找玉戒指。

But the ring was nowhere to be found. Finally Mama suggested, "Patty, you should help them."

Papa encouraged her, "Yes, we know that you can do it." So Patty thought of a plan!

他们还是找不到玉戒指。最后猪妈妈建议说："派娣，你去帮帮他们。"

猪爸爸也鼓励她："是的，我们知道你一定能做到。"于是，派娣想了一个计划！

That night, as Cousin Dog stood watch, Patty dozed off and started to snore loudly.

"Why can't you sleep right?" whined Auntie Horse.

But Patty kept on snoring.

那天晚上，狗表哥正在当更，派娣打起了瞌睡並开始大声打鼾。

“为什么你不能好好地睡觉？”马阿姨嘀咕着说。

可派娣仍然继续打鼾。

Watching Patty enjoy her sleep, a tired Cousin Dog decided to get some rest too.

But when he left, Patty opened her eyes and tiptoed closer to the pigpen's gate.

看着派娣舒服睡觉的样子，
疲倦的狗表哥也决定休息一下。

但是当他离开了，派娣睁开了眼睛，
躡手躡脚地走到栅栏边。

Then Patty rolled on the ground and coated herself with mud.
"Why are you getting so dirty?" bleated Auntie Sheep.

Next Patty crouched as low as she could under the gate's bottom rail.

然后派娣在泥浆里滚了一身泥。
"为什么你弄得这么肮脏？"
羊阿姨哼了一声。

接下来派娣尽可能蹲在栅栏底部。

She squeezed, squeaked, and slithered. Finally she slipped out! Auntie Horse and Sheep gasped with surprise.

Curious to learn what Patty was up to, Uncle Ox tagged along.

她挤啊挤，发出吱吱聲。终于滑了出去！
马阿姨和羊阿姨惊讶地发出叫声。

牛大叔一路跟着，他想知道派娣到底想做什么。

In his haste, Farmer Wu had dropped one of his gloves outside her pen. After sniffing it, Patty noticed something else in the air,

**"That is a strange smell."**
So Patty followed the scent.

之前，农夫老吴匆忙中在猪圈外头
留下了一只手套。派娣闻了闻手套以后，
发现空气中有一股不一样的气味说：
“这是一种奇怪的气味。”
于是派娣跟着这股气味去。

Around the corner of the barn, she found the farm's compost heap. It was piled high with leftover plants and vegetables of all sorts. "Why are you still so hungry?" grunted Uncle Ox.

在谷仓的拐角处，她发现了农场的堆肥。上面堆满了各种各样的剩菜和植物。
“你为什么还这么饿？”牛叔叔哼了一声。

**"This is it!"** exclaimed Patty and she began digging through the mound.

She eyed apples, apricots, and artichokes.

"就在这里！派娣兴奋地大叫，然后她开始挖土堆。她发现了苹果，杏子和朝鲜蓟。

Then she bumped into beans, broccoli, and bitter melon.

然后她翻出豆子，西兰花和苦瓜。

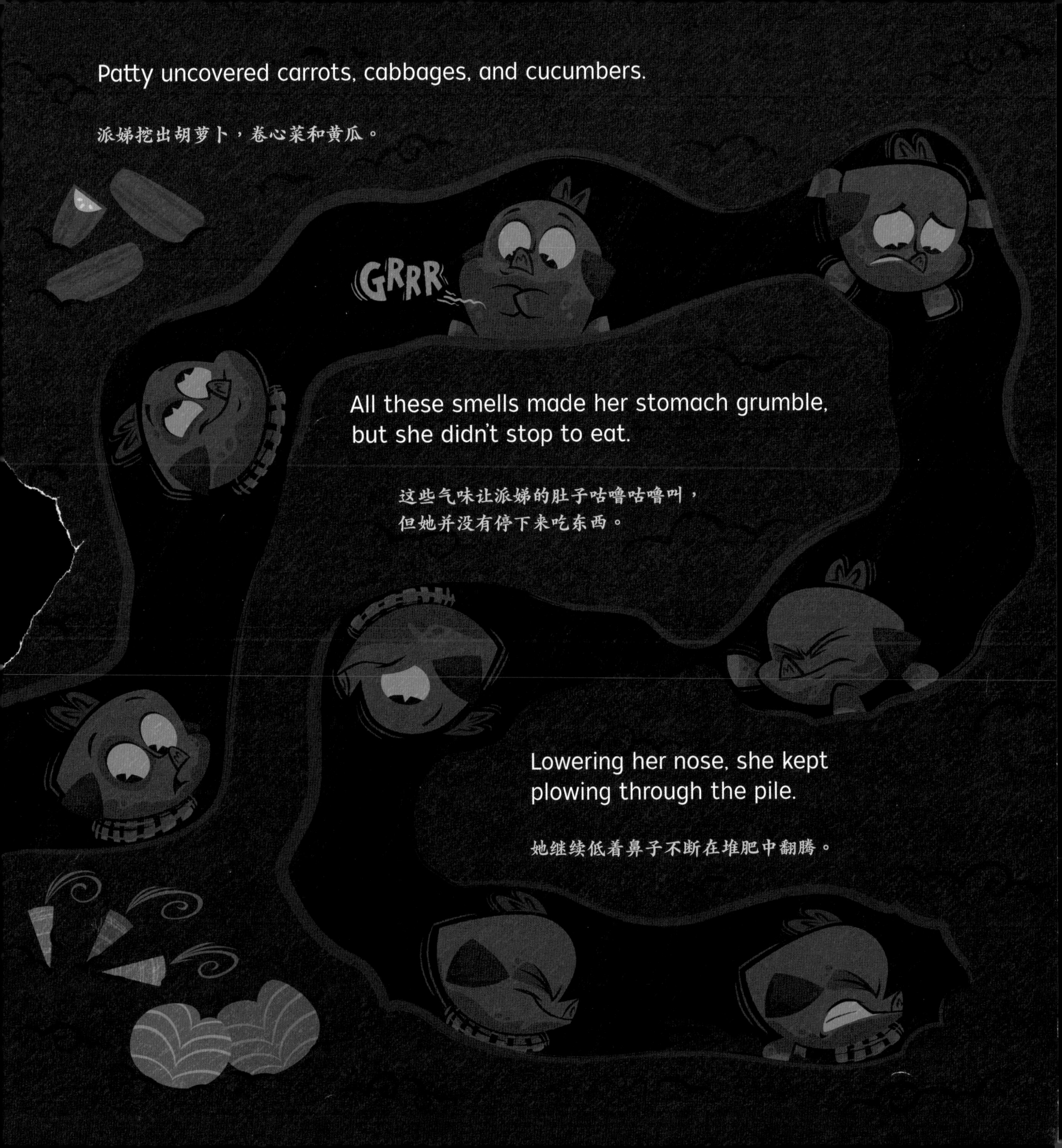


Patty uncovered carrots, cabbages, and cucumbers.

派娣挖出胡萝卜，卷心菜和黄瓜。

All these smells made her stomach grumble, but she didn't stop to eat.

这些气味让派娣的肚子咕噜咕噜叫，
但她并没有停下来吃东西。

Lowering her nose, she kept plowing through the pile.

她继续低着鼻子不断在堆肥中翻腾。

Finally Patty discovered something that wasn't food at all.

She squealed, **"I've found it!"**

Hearing her cry, everybody rushed out to the barn.

派娣终于发现了不属于食物的东西。

她尖叫说："我找到了！"

大家听到她的叫声，都冲向谷仓。

They were amazed that Patty had been so helpful.

"I must have lost my ring after I dropped my glove," marveled Farmer Wu.

"You are very sensible indeed," admitted Cousin Dog.

大家对派娣的帮助表示很惊讶。

"我一定是在丢掉手套的时候，
弄丢了我的戒指，"农夫老吴惊叹说。

"你真的很聪明，"
狗表哥不得不承认。

Afterwards, Farmer Wu would let Patty out of the pen wherever she pleased. Patty even got to go into the house as long as she took a bath beforehand.

這事之后，农夫老吴让派娣自由进出猪圈，
还答应派娣可以去他家，只是記得去之前要洗洗澡。

Mama and Papa Pig were proud of their little piglet.
No one complained anymore about Patty's manners, and everyone agreed it was a remarkable Year of the Pig.

猪妈妈和猪爸爸为他们的小猪感到骄傲。再也没有人说派娣没有规矩了，
大家都认为这是一个了不起的猪年。

# 豬

**Pig**

**1923, 1935, 1947, 1959, 1971, 1983, 1995, 2007, 2019, 2031**

People born in the Year of the Pig are warm, sociable, and sincere. They are resilient, inquisitive, and intelligent. But they can be impulsive, sensitive, and stubborn. Though they may seem to take their time and enjoy themselves, the generosity and courage of pigs are qualities to treasure!

在猪年出生的人，性格热情、善于交际、待人真诚。他们做事有弹性，对事物充满好奇，头脑聪明。但是有时会比较冲动、敏感而且固执。虽然他们似乎很会花时间享受自己，但猪的慷慨和勇敢却是值得赞赏的！


*Enjoy more fun bilingual stories by Ying Chang Compestine!*

CONTRA COSTA COUNTY LIBRARY

31901064086186

"Compestine's lively, original folktale is filled with action, noise, and humor, nicely captured in the detailed, cut-paper illustrations that resemble stained glass. An excellent choice for read-alouds."

–*ALA Booklist*